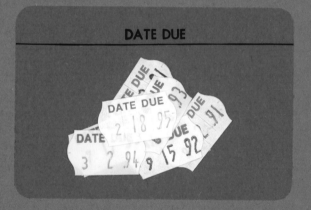

DATE DUE

ABCDEFGHIJKLMNOPQRSTUVWXYZ

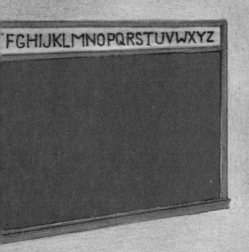

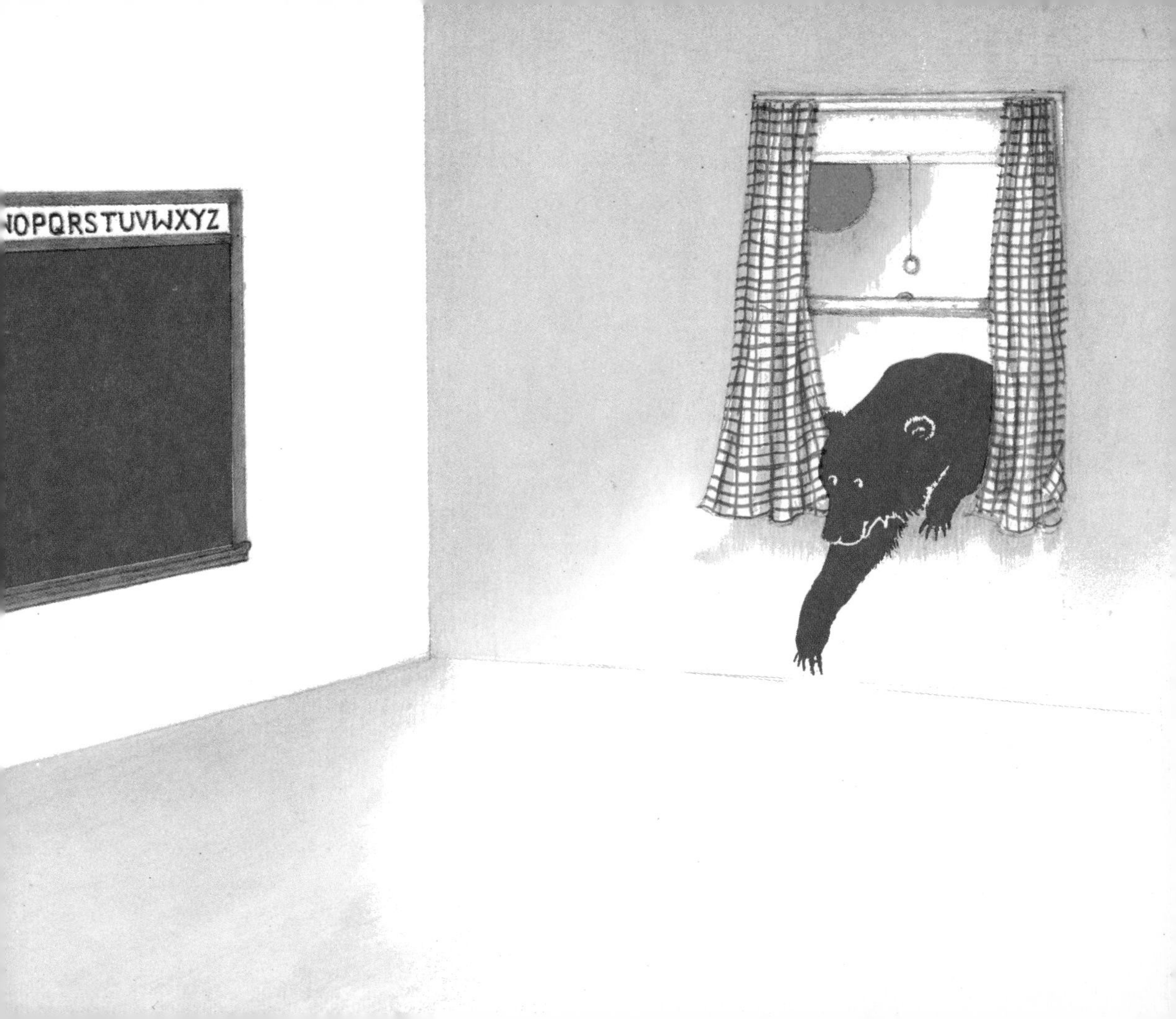
NOPQRSTUVWXYZ

Come on, sleepyhead!
Let's go play.

Hi, fellas. What's the matter?

We're scared. There's a giant monster loose.

Last night it stole all the goldfish out of my pond.

And it took a big jar of my mom's honey right off the windowsill. It must have arms ten feet long!

And it took all the blueberries in our garden.
It left giant footprints all over.

Let's search for him. My bear can help, and
he'll protect us from the monster.

See, there are the prints. Maybe it's a dinosaur!
Or a lion! Or a gorilla!

Look, Anthony, they're as big as your bear's.

Yikes! They're just *like* your bear's.

My gosh! They *are* your bear's.

They are not! They couldn't be.
He was in my room with me all night.

We're not playing with *you* anymore, Anthony.
Your bear is just a crook! A robber! A thief!

Let's get the police and have him put in jail.

Those liars!

What? They're not lying?
You really took those things?

But why didn't you tell me?

Really? You thought I might not like you anymore?
I might even give you away?

I would *never* do that.
Don't you know I'm your *friend*?

But you're not in the woods, you know.
You can't just help yourself to other people's things.
Let's go return them.

We can't? You ate them *all*?
Oh, gosh, we're in trouble.

No money to pay them back.
What can we do?

You want to try? You never drew before.
Well, I'll get some chalk.

But, Anthony, I only had six fish.
There are eleven here.

Maybe one had babies.

I guess you're not so good at counting.
Well, nobody's good at everything.